Mucumber McGee

AND THE
LUNCH LADY'S LIVER

written and illustrated by

PATRICK LOEHR

Katherine Tegen Books
An Imprint of HarperCollins Publishers

Also by Patrick Loehr

Mucumber McGee
and the Half-Eaten Hot Dog

For Wesley, Dad, Mike, Jeff,
and the Grandpas

In a dismal old schoolhouse
down by the sea,
there was a young boy
named Mucumber McGee.

Lunch had begun,
and Mucumber was late!
He took the last napkin
and took the last plate.

"I hope there is food!
Or what will I do?
Perhaps there are hot dogs,
or maybe fondue."

Mucumber was worried.
He glanced all around.
He looked for some food,
but none could be found.

He approached the lunch lady
with great apprehension,
because she had warts
and severe hypertension.

"Mucumber, you're late!
Do you know what this means?
I have no more beef stew
and no more green beans!

But thankfully, Mucumber,
I do have something here—
a very special recipe,
a meal I hold dear."

"It may be brown and lumpy,
but please, make no mistake—
the flavor is delicious.
Enjoy your LIVER CAKE!"

She put the liver on his plate.
But Mucumber wasn't pleased.
It looked like an old bowling shoe
and smelled like rotten cheese.

"Liver cake?" Mucumber asked.
"I don't mean to be rude,
but I'm afraid I cannot eat
this strange and smelly food."

The lunch lady was shocked—
this made her quite uptight.
"Listen here, Mucumber,
you must eat every bite."

Mucumber took his liver cake
and sat down in his chair.
His sister stood behind him—
she couldn't help but stare.

"What is THAT, Mucumber,
that clump upon your plate?
MY lunch looked much better,
and MY lunch tasted great."

"The lady called it liver cake.
I must eat every bite.
But suddenly I'm feeling weak.
I've lost my appetite."

"Don't you know, Mucumber,
the lunch lady is mean.
She told you it is liver,
but it might be a SPLEEN!

Some say she is dangerous,
and you should be afraid.
I wouldn't trust her cooking
or eat that food she made."

"You know she gets quite angry
at students who are late.
I've heard she cooks up rats and frogs
and serves them on a plate!"

"Goodness!" said Mucumber.
"My worst fears have come true.
I must now eat a stinky glob
of unknown lumpy goo."

The lunch lady was watching.
Mucumber felt her stare.
He saw her grab her cleaver
and wave it in the air.

"She's threatening me," Mucumber said.
"Now what will I do?
If I don't eat this liver cake,
I'll wind up in her stew!"

Against his better judgment
Mucumber took a bite.
He put the liver in his mouth
and clenched his teeth down tight.

Mucumber's taste buds came alive.
The liver was delicious!
It tasted simply wonderful.
So fresh—and so nutritious!

Mucumber savored every slice,
each morsel, bit, and crumb.
He waved at the lunch lady,
and then stuck up his thumb.

Now everything was perfect
in that schoolhouse by the sea.
So, children, please listen,
now listen to me.

If your lunch is scary
and lumpy and brown,
if the smell makes you grimace
and the color makes you frown . . .

Don't worry—
it won't taste as bad as it looks.
Because lunch ladies are usually . . .

very good cooks.

Thank you:
Alice Martel, Katherine Tegen,
Martha Rago, and Emily Lawrence,
for your vision, insight, and commitment!

Mucumber McGee and the Lunch Lady's Liver

Copyright © 2008 by Patrick Loehr

Manufactured in China.

www.harpercollinschildrens.com

Library of Congress Cataloging-in-Publication Data is available.
ISBN 978-0-06-082330-6 (trade bdg.)
ISBN 978-0-06-082331-3 (lib. bdg.)

Designed by Martha Rago
1 2 3 4 5 6 7 8 9 10 ❖ First Edition